THE BEGINNING OF THE END

SHREEYA SHARMA

Made with ♥ on the Notion Press Platform
www.notionpress.com

TO THE ONE WHO FEARS BUT DOES'NT SAY TO THE ONE WHO'S LURKING IN THE SHADOWS WAITING AS TIME GOES BY ..... TICK TOCK TICK TOCK. IS WHAT YOU SEE REAL HOW CAN YOU BE SURE THAT IT ACTUALLY EXISTS ? OR ARE YOUR EYES JUST DECIEVING YOU ? DO YOU EVEN KNOW WHO YOU ARE ? AND WHO YOU ARE MEANT TO BE ?

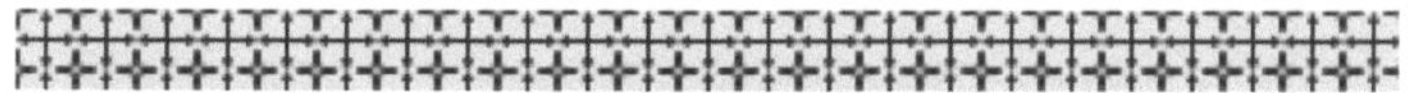

TO ALL THE READERS WHO ARE ON THEIR PATH FOR SELF - DISCOVERY

WITH LOVE

Contents

Contents

Foreword

THE AUTHOR ON A PATH TO SELF DISCOVERY AND AMAZEMENT . THIS BOOK SHOULD BE READ BECAUSE IT INFORMS US ABOUT ALL THE CHALLENGING ACTIVITIES FACED BY A 16 YEAR OLD HUMAN BEING .

Acknowledgements

THANK YOU EVERYONE FOR ENCOURAGING AND SUPPORTING ME TILL THE END . A SPECIAL THANK YOU TO MY PARENTS WHO HAVE BEEN A PILLAR OF SUPPORT IN MY LIFE .

CHAPTER ONE

THE MEET

It began like any other normal day my so i'm Lara Jones and my sister is luna so luna and I were pretty close together like any other normal sisters we fought a lot but that's a different story, anyway so Luna was 4 years older to me and we both were going to be transfered in a new school as we were moing to a different country we shifted in to a new house everything seemed to be going great .....

Until we met Brielle she was charming and very nice to both of us our bond grew deeper but whenever we visited her house we always got this strange feeling that something was off but we never really could understand what. Brielle was fearless there was this " haunted mansion " (according to us you'll soon know why)don't ask me why it always has to be a house! The first time I saw it , I was only six it was night and I was playing in

my grandad's garden and there was a forest nearby it was so close that I could litterly see those awful bats it was terrifying but then I heard this really weird noise coming from the forest it was like the forest was calling me I followed the sound and found myself in the middle of a circle surrounded by huge tall trees and bushes .

THE MEET

I was scared out of my skin but determined to find where the voice came from I went on ..... I was litterly freaking out ! My eyes were closed don't ask me "why" I was six okay?! When I suddenly bumped in to something at first I thought that it's just a normal tree but when I felt around I realised it was much more than a tree I was dying of curosity but i dared not to open my eyes but then there was this voice again .....

It was like a song an extremely creepy song I opened my eyes there was this purple smog I screamed uncontrollably and I saw a face smeared in the fog and then someone or something gabbed my leg! I think that's when I fainted it was too much to handle for a six year old ! I woke up to find myself in my grandad's house safe and sound and not eaten up by anything . Luna and my grandad noticed that I was not playing n the garden and immediately started to search me they found me unconscious in the woods at about 2:00 in the night and brought me here they were quite concerned but I was fine and told them the whole story it sent shivers down their spine my sister hugged me and soon we shifted out of that apartment to another house and since then I have never dared to go there or even talk about it !

And now it has been 10 years since it all happened and I still remember that day vividly it was as if it was just yestarday I was I was freaking out only talking about it ! But of course Brielle wanted to visit that place and find out the truth I was like are you crazy?! She said that maybe I was so scared that I starting having hallucations and everything that I saw was just a trick of the mind . I know it can't be imaginary I.....I...I saw it! "Are you sure though?" Brielle asked . I had no answer she had made me question everything that had happened in the past was it all really fake ? What if it all was just a dream ? Had I worried my family members for nothing ? I needed answers so I allowed Brielle to go even though she didn't exactly need my permisson but anyway, Brielle even insisted that I go with here and what can I say that girl is very persuasive! I chimed but I told her that if we're doing this let's do it the proper way .

THE MEET

Even though Brielle was fearless we still had to maintain caution ! So next we packed everything we needed to survive the wild and of course food a tent and other stuff that we needed to investigate we were only going to stay in the woods for one night but we had to stay prepared ! My dad's in the millatry and she told us to be careful and she also told us to come back as soon as we sense any trouble which I hope by God's grace does'nt happen! But if it does I'll be running like a rocket ! When I got out of my house Brielle was already waiting for me .

She said that it was about a 2 kilometer walk from my house to the forest so we better get moving . I was glad that by the time we reached the forest it was still daylight and the sun was still shining brightly it was about 2:00 in the afternoon and we had our lunch when Brielle took a compass out of her bag and started to check it and soon said that" we had to head North it's said to be the most haunted place in the forest " Brielle said . But the place where I experienced the things is East so we have to head East not North don't be ridiculous Brielle you're obviously wrong " I said which was astonishing because Brielle was ususally correct but that does’nt mean that she can never be wrong right ? Brielle looked up on the information again and she could‘nt believe her eyes this time ,she said that she must have read it wrong or something but now it says East! Give me that I said snatching the phone from her , sure enough it said East .We both just decided to go East and forget this ever happened . Brielle told me that it was about a 3 mile hike from here to the place where you saw had all those " strange happenings " she teased . Well I’m sure if it happened to you , it would'nt be funny ! I replied . Whatever, hey , we better get moving we gotta reach there before Nightfall ! she said .

By the time we headed off it was already 2:45 we were going pretty behind on schedule I could tell that even Brielle was quite tense and walking faster then usual but since the path was jagged and rocky she was forced to slow down and watch her step on our way we passed a small lake I don’t know how it’s possible but that lake had crystal clear water, I could literally see my own reflection shimmering in the light! It felt majestic !

CHAPTER TWO

THE PAST ....

I noticed that this forest was different from the ones that I had ever seen and I'm telling you I've seen a lot of forests the wilderness ,the air ,the trees everything was so ...so....unique about it , it was as if the forest was actually calling out to me . While we were hiking we stumbeled across a phoenix oh and boy was it angry! I thought that we were done for ! Oh god save us ! Brielle screamed so loud that I thought the president would be able to hear her ! But the phoenix kneeled down before me I know this sounds crazy but believe this is what happened ! I.... I.. think it wants us to climb on it's back !? I said with uncertainity . Brielle stop shouting ! I screamed at her she finaly calmed down. Let's just do what the phoenix is telling us to do . Oh yeah, sure, let's just risk our lives following a phoenix! Lara get ahold of youself do you even know what you're saying ?! Brielle shouted . Brielle I need you to listen I have a really good idea about this I just need you to trust me okay I said as I climbed on to the phoenix's back . Besides phoenix are known to be friendly creatures I send as I extended my hand towards her while telling her to just climb the phoenix and remain calm Brielle climbed on the phoenix . Uhh ....Lara is'nt the phoenix an enxtinct species!?

I was frozen in my tracks , the Phoenix had started to fly in the air . I mean there are still some Phoenix left in Arizona , I said but this isn't Arizona ! Brielle said . Brielle I don't think there's much we can do now let's just trust the Phoenix I said and with this the Phoenix gave us a really eery smile and descended towards some trees that were placed in a circular manner ...... Hey I know this place ! I shouted but Brielle didn't hear me Brielle what's wrong ? I asked her . Lara have you noticed that this phoenix doesn't have wings and is still flying ? Brielle asked . I got a closer look at the phoenix and I realized this wasn't a phoenix at all.....

It was ......nothing! We were floating on thin air ! The phoenix was just an illusion! Wait a second , Lara how is it that we're simply floating in the air!? Wait a second Brielle we ain't floating in thin air we're not riding a phoenix but it seems to be some sort of girl

? A girl made of fire? Excuse me miss do you mind landing I'm getting airsick Brielle told the phoenix-girl . I sighed and the Phoenix - girl said in a musical voice that" we're just going to be landing ,you too do not know what fate has in store for you "

Right, okay wasn't that like way too dramatic ? Brielle teased I sighed.... again as the phoenix rised again.....

THE PAST........

So, Phoenix-girl do you have a name? I asked as politely as I could "I'm known as Ava" she answered . So may we call you Ava ? Brielle asked on my behalf ." Yes you may" Ava replied . So where and why are you taking us ? Lara do you remember what you saw in these woods when you were six? Ava asked me , yes of course I do that's the main reason why we're here! I said . Well Lara a full moon is a magical time in these woods it's the time when evil lurks free , humans I mean you , Lara you should'nt have ventured alone in the forest at that time , Lara what you saw was the evil trying to capture you the purple fog that you saw was the evil , well let me make this more clear the evil can take many forms and since it was a full moon night it became a werewolf that's the face you saw in the purple fog and it was the werewolf that grabbed see Lara and Brielle you may not know this but werewolves can sense power and energy and that's what he sensed in you Lara , which is why it wanted to suck your power and energy and then ultimately you would have died within minutes ,said Ava .

Me and Brielle were too stunned to speak , I slowly found my voice again and then spoke , but I still don't get it , if the werewolf could have killed me why didn't it? Well Lara that's because as soon as the werewolf grabbed your leg you fainted and the werewolf must have thought that you were dead and well , if a person has powers and they die the powers disappear...... Ava said .Woah that's some epic adventure ! Brielle said , wait a second! What powers ? I don't have any powers! I told Ava. Exactly , Lara how long have you known your mother for ? Well she passed away when I was young , well if I'm to be specific when I was just one she ....died . Lara do you know how she died ? I'm not so sure my dad told me that she passed away in some sort of accident . No Lara ,your mother when she was young , just about the same age that you are now , she had a strong connection with this forest and one day when she was wandering around the woods looking for mushrooms, she touched an ancient tree , that tree is known to be the oldest tree in the forest when your mother touched it she got the ancient powers of the tree and she used those powers for good she created an alternate dimension where it would be safe for werewolves and other mystical creatures to live but you remember I told you about "the evil" well , your mother sent the evil inside the alternate dimension and locked so that no creatures could come outside to the human world , I mean this world and no humans can go inside it either but unfortunately this consumed all her powers and well , and as I said earlier the evil can take many or practically any form so 12 years later when you were born and just 1 year old the evil took the

THE PAST........

form of your mother's worst enemy and challenged her to battle but like I said earlier she had lost her powers and was now she very weak, but she still wanted to fight so she put up her most bravest face of all time and faced her opponent but then I have absloutely no clue how you Lara got in Andrielle's hand and - , wait hold on Ava ! Who's Andrielle now ? I asked. That's the name of your mother's worst enemy , Andrielle. Now don't interupt me when I'm speaking Lara and listen carefully , now where was I ? Ah yes.

So Lara the battle was going on in the living room of your own house, exactly where you live today so Lara you crawled in to the living room since you were a baby , you had no idea what was going on so you started crying , and then Andrielle noticed you , so obviously she took advantage of it and grabbed you in her hands and started to threaten you mother , Olivia, oh she had such a beautiul name , well anyway , Andrielle told Olivia to sacrifice herself or else ......So then obviously she sacrificed herself in order to protect you Lara , it was a life or death situation for your mother she chose death. Ava stopped speaking for a few moments , then when Brielle asked her well what happened after that ? How did she actualy die? . Yeah Ava you said she sacrificed herself to Andrielle but how did Andrielle kill her ? How did Andrielle kill her ? I asked I was dying to know , I was finaly going to learn something about my mom!

CHAPTER THREE

THE MYSTIC REALM

Okay I'll tell you what happened but first tell me Lara , how did you get that scar , close to your eye? Well, I'm not sure I got it when I was about....one! Ava is my scar related to the battle ?! I shouted at her. Ava nodded and sighed again Lara you know nothing about your mother do you ? Ava asked me I gave her my puppy eyes and she just smiled and said well after your mother decided to sacrifice herself Andrielle teleported them both to a land where she stabbed your mother in the back with a sword and ..... killed her........

We all were silent for about an hour when Brielle screamed , Ava why does my phone say that we've been travelling for three whole days ?! Ava my parents must be worried sick about me! Oh and one more thing I don't remember you telling us about where we're going !? So if you don't mind I would like to know where you're taking us!? Brielle calm down , time works differently here 3 days of this world is only 3 minutes of your world , and we've reached Ava said as she was landing ,in front of us was some kind of portal . You remeber the alternate dimension that I said your mother created ? Well , this is it girls , Ava said . But Ava why are we here ? The werewolf I told you about I mean the evil , it lurks you have to find a way to defeat it basically try to make the evil take any living form so that you can end it once and for all. Try to make it take the form of a werewolf because werewolves are known to be weak okay? Nope , not okay I said , Yeah we are so not doing that said Brielle, anyway I understand that her mother was a part of all this but why me ?! Brielle do you really think if you wouldn't have convinced Lara to come here all this would ever have happened ? Ava replied . Hmm , sounds about right said Brielle . Okay so now you two better skeddadle time's running up . Come on Brielle let's go I told her we said bye to Ava and started our journey.

THE MYSTIC REALM

Ugh this place smells like a swamp Brielle said , yeah I know I replied , wait what's that shiny thing glowing over there ? Where ? asked Brielle. Over there ! Why do I have this feeling that it's coming toward us ?! I shouted . Oh my gosh! Brielle it's a stampede run! We both ran for our lives but then there were leopards leading all whatever other animals were there , I seriously do not even want to talk about it ! But then the question arises how were we going to outrun them ?! The animals got closer and closer ......but then the strangest thing happened the animals went right through us it was as if we were'nt even there ! And we were there wondering about what just happened . Oh I get it ! It was an illusion! Lara the stampede that happened now wasn't real it was all in our minds ! Brielle look what I found! It's a paper on it was written :

"I am born in fear, raised in the truth, and I come to my own indeed. When comes a time that I'm called forth, I come to serve the cause of need. TICK TOCK SUN SET ."

Okay so now what do we do ?and who sent us this letter ? Suddenly Brielle noticed something and said Lara we're in danger we have to leave this place right now! Or else we'll be dead before the sun sets !Woah girl steady how do you know of all this ? And how can you be so sure ? Well first things first whoever wrote this message is pretty dangerous itself , second Lara don't uou get it ?! The message is written in blood ! I immediately dropped the paper but the blood was in my hands I screamed and fanited 17 hours later I woke up to the sound of my phone ringing I didn't pay much attention to it but then at 7 in the morning I froze in terror there was a strange figure who had this mysterious weapon with him or her or it ?! It was surrounded with a black cloud . It was looking right at me or atleast I thought it was I looked in to it's face only to realise he does'nt have one ! I was petrified! I was too frozen to move . Suddenly my head started spinning , I started getting dizzy I could hear Brielle's muffled scream it was as if the 'thing' was trying to quiet her. The last thing that I remember seeing before I fainted again, was that it was wearing a strange bracelet . The bracelet was made up of skulls. I remember trying to run in to the forest , blood everywhere , the thing laughng , Brielle shouting and then .....

CHAPTER FOUR

FEAR OF DEATH

Lara wake up! Huh? Brielle we need to leave this place immediately ! We'll die! I said . Lara is everything alright ?she asked . I told her what happened in the night she laughed and said it was probably just a dream. No! Brielle, no! It was not a dream I could feel it's presence around me! It's too real to be fake . I need you to relax , you're fine . As we walked more I realized that this was exactly like the place I had seen in my dream ..... maybe it wasn't a dream after all ....

I was too nervous to tell Brielle I was afraid that she would just .....pop out. Brielle told me that she'll be back after investigating this particular tree . She said there was something "suspicous" about it . I slapped my forehead and let her go . I sat on a log of wood and began to think when something pulled my hair from behind and started to drag me along the ground I resisted a lot but when I figured it was the same person who almost killed me last night... Then sudddenly I remembered the message :

> *"I am born in fear, raised in the truth, and I come to my own indeed. When comes a time that I'm called forth, I come to serve the cause of need. TICK TOCK SUN SET "*

CHAPTER FOUR

FEAR OF DEATH

FEAR OF DEATH

The letter was written by death itself! It was the darkness! He wanted to kill me ! He disappeared! Suddenely Brielle appeared. I gasped for breath , and told her everything . Brielle calmed me down and told me that she found a map of this place and on the back of the map it was written it dried blood that: The place is called Deadwood and there are 7 places here reserved for the devil it hunts and kills those who disturb him in his territory have you noticed that the time when you get these visions it's exactly 7'o'clock, said brielle. Oh I get it now . Breille those weren;t visions they were real , I explained it to her . Yeah I get it now she said .

vision or true ?

FEAR OF DEATH

I broke down sobbing bitterely . Brielle isn't the one who usually gives pep talks but the advice she gave me that day has changed my entire life I remember her saying it crystal clear :

"Life isn't fair Lara god does'nt sometimes give you what you want not because you don't deserve it but because you deserve better I know you're thinking of your sister right now and wishing she was here to show you the right path but she's not here and if you ever want to see her again then , I need you to fight Lara if not for youself then for your family , your friends , for me and most importantly for that angel inside you !"

CHAPTER FIVE

THE CAVE OF THE ONE......

Okay I said getting back to my senses . Lara there's a place in this map called ' the cave of the one ' I paused waiting for her to go ahead when she didn't I realised ,that was the full name ' the cave of the one 'oh, come on ! Brielle you're not saying that we have to go there it's 19 kilometers away ! Lara we have travelled 46 kilometers so far I'm sure that these 19 kilometers are gonna be a piece of cake . Easy for you to say , you litterly won the 8 kilometer marathon just a couple of weeks ago ! I came in last ! I told Brielle.

Of course Brielle didn't listen to me and rather cruelly dragged me along with her on an 11 mile hike to the cave . To make matters worse we had to pass through jagged mountains ,multiple rivers and waterfulls to reach the heart of the place where the cave

was located ! Oh Lara! stop exaggerating things ! Brielle told me. Okay so I maybe had exaggerated some things but anyway the journey was still not a piece of cake !

THE CAVE OF THE ONE ....

I was exhausted after walking just a kilometer and looked like a dried up flower . Brielle on the other hand looked like she had just woken up and had a cappuccino with a shot of expresso! I had come to accept the fact that she was the leader now , anway I was so exhausted after running five whole kiometers that I was litterly walking slower then a mouse . So, to kill some time I asked Brielle ,why we were going there ? She told me that maybe there's a chance that the evil that we have to kill resides there and if it does then we could try to defeat and kill it . I mean the chance of us getting in danger 76% but I'm sure that we'll be just fine she said flashing me a smile . I sighed , there was nothing in this whole entire galaxy that could change Brielle, I thought to myself and smiled .

Brielle had told me that we had to reach the cave before nightfall because venturing in the forest at night could be dangerous . I have no idea what she means by "dangerous" because we had stayed alive for two whole nights in this forest . What's the worst thing that could possibly happen?

THE CAVE OF THE ONE

CHAPTER SIX

THE PHANTOM HORSE

Ahh yes , no sooner had I said that ,when it started raining . Brielle gave me a questoning look , as if to say " you got your answer now ?" I had no idea what to say so I just smiled nervously . I have got to learn not to say that , I thought. So we continued walking in the rain . To be honest walking in the rain was actually much better then walking in the heat I know I sound crazy but the raindrops falling slowly on my face , felt so relaxing and peaceful . I was surprised that in a place that was practically like a haunted house it wasn't raining ghosts or anything. After we had finished 16 kilometers we sat down to take a breath . That was when I noticed something made up of pure silver coming towards us...it came closer and closer getting bigger and bigger ....It was a horse! Not just any ordianry horse it was a phantom horse! But it didn't harm us in in fact it seemed

rather friendly we both were worn out so when the phantom horse offered a ride on her back to the cave , we without any hesitation accepted . It began to ride so fact that we had to hold on to our hats so that it wouldn't fly away!

SHREEYA SHARMA

The Phantom Horse

CHAPTER SEVEN

DESTINY OR MISTAKE?

As soon as we reached the cave the horse disappeared in to the shadows and if I‘m honest after all that me and Brielle went through I’m not even surprised but as soon as we stepped in to the cave I knew we had either made a huge mistake or we’re challenging the devil . I had seen a lot of astonishing things in this place that is called Deadwood but the most astonishing thing was that in was both night and day! The sun was on one part of the cave, which was all bright and sunny and smelled like lavender and the moon was on the other side of the cave which was dark , creepy and it must have stunk to high heaven in there , it smelled like rotten mashed potatoes and gave out a horrible , horrible stench .

Me and Brielle both just stared at the cave wondering what to do next . Then Brielle looked at me and said that we should go towards the dark part of the cave .

INSIDE THE CAVE

DESTINY OR MISTAKE?

I shook my head as if to say no because so far whatever we had been through in this world it was nothing what it seems like it was always some sort of an illusion . So I told Brielle that I think that we should go towards the part that seems ‘ light and friendly ’ because nothing is what it appears to be I said in a dramatic tone . But then Brielle could also be right I mean ,what kind of monster stays in a place that smells like lavender?!

I think it was pretty obvious what had to be done now .... We would have to split up there was no other option...... If we both went together then we could lose precious time and we only had until sunset to kill the evil and the devil .Which is why we both told each other to be safe and I headed down towards the light and friendly path .Which is, I hoped was light and friendly and not dark and scary.

Was it my destiny or just a huge mistake ?

THE STRANGE MESSAGE

I began to start my journey my legs were paining so much fron walking all day , oh how I wished if Ava (The phoenix-girl) was here ! As soon as I said that Ava magically apearred and to be honest I was so relieved that I won't have to walk anymore. Ava! I shouted with immense joy. Ava told me to climb on her back . I did as she told because over time I had come to trust Ava . But, this time there was something wrong . The color of her wings had started to fade...... , it had started to turn in a deep black sort of color . Ava noticed me staring at her wings that's when she explained to me that "it was because of the evil , the evil had taken the form of a devil that you had been seeing , Lara . " Ava told me. That's when I noticed that there was a change in her voice when she spoke the next few lines " Lara you are in great danger , something you never expected , your greatest fear will come to light today. Which is why Lara I need you to not have an emotional attachment with anyone who is in this world . Lara because today something will happen that can be the cause of your life and death..." Ava told me in a deep and mysterious voice that I had never heard from her mouth when she spoke to me .

Okay , wait Ava you told me to not get emotionally attached to someone and also not to trust anyone in this world , so..... does that include you? I was shaking with fear while asking this I wasn't scared but I also wasn't sure if she wasn't the devil (it could change forms remember?!) Lara do you see something like a symbol or a tattoo sorta thing on my hand ? Ava asked me . It was the first time that I had glanced down to look at her arm . The tattoo or symbol , whatever , contained all the four elements of nature : Water , Fire, Air and Earth. In the middle there was some sort of strange symbol which had a circle and a bunch of triangles inside it and it was just so strange! I asked Ava what the symbol meant in the middle and that is how she began her one hour long speech and I pretty much understood everything in the first line

THE STRANGE MESSAGE

THE STRANGE SYMBOL

CHAPTER EIGHT

THE DAZZLING RUBY

Lara whoever you see with this symbol is trustworthy because the symbol in between was your mother's symbol she gave it to us before she died . Ava explained. Wait, what do you mean by "us" ? I mean that I'm not the only one who you can trust, there are thirteen different kinds of creauters in this forest who are trustworthy . With these last words after she spoke an arrow flew towards me but Ava stopped it . Ava fell to the ground she was groaning in pain and agony . Find .....t-the r-ruby! Her last words . What ruby ?where? how ? me ? I had a bunch of questions but before she could answer any of them .She stopped breathing..... Ava I shouted tearfully. She had helped me a lot through this mission . She died protecting me! I thought...

So I set off on my mission to find the ruby through which I will kill the evil that had taken the form of the devil that I had been

seeing in my visions !For the first time in my life my mind was crystal clear I knew what I had to ! I would not let Ava's sacrifice go in vain ! When I started to walk I saw something shimmering in the light.... could it be .....? I wondered as soon as I saw it I started running towards it but when I came closer I only saw a huge waterfall . What? But it makes no sense! I'm sure the light was coming from here !

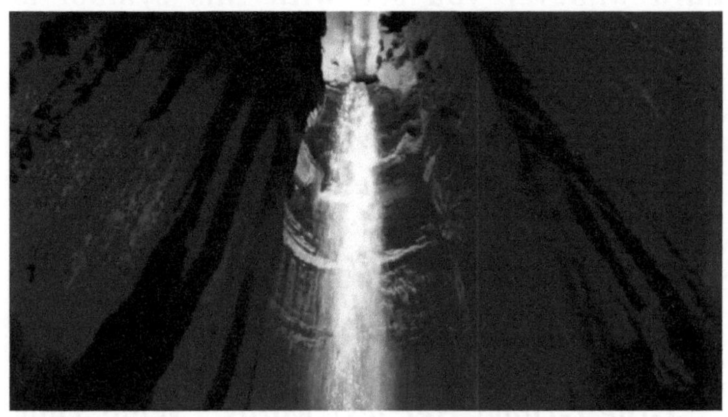

THE MYSTERIOUS LIGHT

THE DAZZLING RUBY

Could it be that the entrance to the ruby was inside the waterfall? I asked myself. Hmm , well there's only one way to find out ! I ran towards the waterfall with all of my remaining strength! And , sure enough I was right ! The entrance was right inside the waterfall ! And inside was a big dazzling, shimmering ruby ! As soon as I touched the ruby it started shining even brighter I saw a vision in my mind .....It was a vision from the future I was with someone he or she was trying to kill me we were somewhere close to a cliff .... then suddenly the vision ended with a picture of a skull bracelet puzzled I found myself near a cliff it was the same cliff that I had seen in my visions ! How was that possible ?! And what about the skull bracelet ?

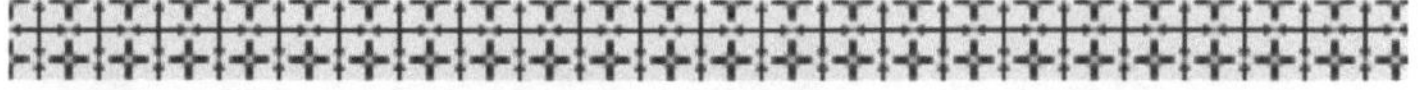

How the hell ? Just when I was finally starting to adjust to this ....this ....this place when I was finally going to get some answers ! I was suddenly teleported to this cliff! Great ! Just Great ! Wait if this was the same cliff in my visions then ? could it be ?

THE OTHER SIDE

THE DAZZLING RUBY

I REALLY HAVE NO CLUE

CHAPTER NINE

BRIELLE?!

Brielle ?! I shouted at her I was confused . What are you doing here ? How did you even get here ? It took me forever to get past that waterfall ! Anyway you will not believe what happened to me today ! I wanted to tell her everything that I did today ! I started to talk but then my voice suddenly trailed off..... The skull bracelet, Brielle was wearing it ! My eyes as big as saucers I could not believe my eyes. Were they deceiving me ? But there was no lie in what was right in front of me .... The skull bracelet it was definitly like the one that I had seen in my visions !

What's wrong ? Why did you stop ? I would love to hear all about your day , alas you would not be alive to do so. Brielle said in a deep and creepy voice . Then all of a sudden as time stood still I saw Brielle my ex- best friend taking out a dagger ! Do not ask what that is for ! I don't even want to think about it ! Was this it ? Was I going to die ? I knew the only way to save myself was to kill Brielle ! But how could I ? She was my best friend ? But I didn't want to die ! This land needed freedom from it's curse ! I have to kill my ex-best friend , Brielle !

BRIELLE HEADING TOWARDS ME WITH A SWORD
!

CHAPTER TEN

MISSON BRIELLE

My mind kept on repeating one thing " Run Lara ! Run! Do you want to die !?" But my heart kept on saying " Lara she's your friend , how can she possibly kill you ?" I tried to console Brielle and gave her a speech about friendship and loyalty . But as Brielle crept closer and closer , my mind won over my heart and I figured out that it would be best to run away for now and I can finish this whole Brielle buisness later after doing some investigation. I thought and ran as fast as the wind as I was running I bumped in to the wolf that I had been trying to find all along , but he looked way to old to even run let alone kill someone !

But then I remembered that Ava had told me that the evil can take many forms ! So what if the evil has not taken any form and is actually Brielle ?! And this old wolf is innocent ? I can't believe I fell in to that witch Brielle's trap ! I thought . Now , Now don't you think that's a little too harsh , dear ? The wolf said . Huh? How did you know what I was thinking? I was thinking it in my mind! I said . Well obviously. The wolf said. Oh my gosh , can you read minds !? That is so cool! The wolf smiled and gestured me to follow him.

THE LONE WOLF

CHAPTER ELEVEN

MISSON BRIELLE

He took me to his home in the woods it was a small cottage but it felt so close to home you see back in Canada my home is surrounded by trees and flowers of different kinds and I alway welcome birds and squirrels in my home sometimes for a snack .So, it felt nice to be at a place in this world which was not creepy and spooky .

I thought to tell the wolf all about my experience with my ex-best friend Brielle . When I was just about to open my mouth to speak . He told me that he already knew everything and he is ready to help me on one condition. I asked him what his condition was . He said that Lara you have a great amount of energy inside you , that energy can be used for defeating Brielle I understand the trauma you must be going through, but Lara put yourself together and fight for good and most importantly for yourself .

I can't help you if you can't help yourself. I didn't understand a word of what he was trying to tell me , all I knew that I had to defeat Brielle and defend this land for which my mother had shed her blood . Lara are you willing to defend our glory ? The wolf whose name was Dave asked me . Yes I said confidentiality. Well then let's start he said . Wait , start what ? I asked I had no clue what he was talking about . Why, your training of course what else ? He said . Whoa whoa whoa training for what exactly?! I asked . You can't just defeat Brielle like that She's mastered spells and magic for years only then was she able to obtain the orb . Dave said . I am so confused now what is this orb ?!

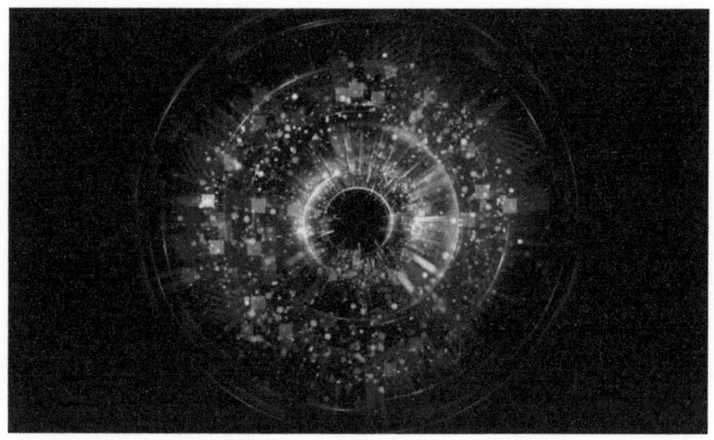

THE ORB

MISSON BRIELLE

THE ORB IS IN BRIELLE 'S HANDS

CHAPTER TWELVE

BELIEVE IN YOURSELF

It looks like a ball but it contains a great deal of power Brielle worked for years just to defeat your mother . Dave said . But why !? What does she get out of it !? What is in it for her !? I asked I NEEDED ANSWERS . Since she was little Brielle has been wanting to destroy the earth and then the entire dimension along with it . But the only person who stood between her plans was your mother, Brielle did manage to kill her but your mother deeply weekend her powers . Which is why she had to wait for 16 years to conquer and destroy the world she mastered a lot of spells and became Powerful which is how she obtained the orb . But then your mother had passed on some of her powers to you , you just need to awaken them and you need to do it within a week or else .....

Dave's voice started to trail off . What will happen after a week ? I asked Dave . Dave gave me a look he was too stunned to speak . And then suddenly when he found his voice back he said I'll tell you when you're ready.. Now come on we only have a week . He said . Okay I replied. I had learned a lot of things in this world but I had also learnt that I should not trust anyone blindly . So I still maintained

caution but I had started to trust him a little

CHAPTER THIRTEEN

BELIEVE IN YOURSELF

FAST FORWARD TO SEVEN DAYS LATER

I had never known that so much energy resided inside of me .The power ... I could feel it bustling inside of me . I was one with the wind , I was one with the strong waved of the ocean , I was one with the anger of fire I was one with the earth I now knew what the symbol that Ava was talking about meant .... It meant world peace

..but if people do not listen and you can't find an option do not let them interfere in your way ....but remember Violence is never

the answer the answer sometimes lies deep without the surface ..

You are ready Dave exclaimed . Remember Lara your powers are useless if you are not calm and confident and always remember the three rules Dave said ... Tride , truth and true I replied . Correct Dave said. Then suddenly I thought I saw something in the bushes I turned around but there was nothing so anyway I turned back to say thanks to Dave for all that he had done for me . There was not a single soul to be seen ... No Dave , No no one there was not a single sign of life anywhere not even Dave's cottage could be seen now . Then suddenly I thought that when you are in desperate need God sends you an angel in disguise to help you to light your path and guide you . I smiled silently as I thought about it and silently thanked Dave and I also thanked God as they had answered my prayer ....But then I noticed that there was something carved on a rock .... It was a message by Dave . It said that " Remember Lara how I always told you that you only have one week to prepare for your battle with Brielle well now it's time to tell you why , after exactly 2 weeks the orb is activated it starts to emit a light of it's own so bright and powerful that it will destroy the whole galaxy, that is why Brielle wanted the orb if you do not break the orb within one week then it will

be THE BEGINNING OF THE END.

BELIEVE IN YOURSELF

THE BEGININNG OF THE END

CHAPTER FOURTEEN

THE BEGINNING OF THE END

And then I hunted for days and nights trying to find Brielle but It was like she had just vanished .....
And then one time when I was sleeping at night I heard a noise and I had learnt from my experience in this place that if you hear a voice at night either it kills you or you kill it . And guess who I found sneaking away with the magical orb . Yup it was Brielle . How can you do this to me Brielle I trusted you ! I shouted at her.

The closest companion is the individual you depend on the most. She's somebody you would trust with your life, your mysteries, and your feelings. You gradually let her into your heart and the trust gathers over the long haul. A bond is framed over those mysteries, a kinship that will last. Never again is anything untouchable, and if that individual ever needs to talk, somebody will be there.

One second can transform everything. The individual you thought was your comrade ends up being a deceiver. The entirety of the mysteries and shared feelings are convoluted and utilized against you. Your shortcomings are played until you separate and are gradually destroyed. At last, the individual is perceived as the truth about. The entirety of the reports and the alleged untruths are valid. You, being the better individual, attempted to look past them, assuming the best about your companion. Yet, when reality comes out and the untruths begin to disentangle, what do you have left? When do you know to release a fellowship and when to hang on? Starting there on, all the trust you once had for your companion is gone and it can never be reconstructed.

THE BEGINNING OF THE END

I said with tears rolling down my cheeks. Sometimes Lara what you want isn't always what you get Brielle said pulling her sword out . In this world and in yours there's one similarity they both have the same slogan : It's either kill or be killed for example today you can either kill or be killed. No you're wrong I replied. It's only under dire circumstances with that I shot an arrow towards her frozen heart luckily for her she managed to be able to Dodge it well not for long I exclaimed. She shot a ball of fire toward me and then I swiftly ran behind her and broke the orb to pieces. Without it her powers would not work and she would eventually grow weak and die but I ain't waiting that long I picked up her sword and like a mighty warrior or as my mother would have done stabbed her in the back with her own sword.Like you said it's either kill or be killed . I said as she breathed her last. I found my way back home and hugged my sister Luna and my grandad and father I was overjoyed to see them ! It felt like eternity. They then asked where Brielle was I showed them the sword which was covered with blood . They didn't ask me anything else .It seemed like they already knew the answer they needed . Anyway so after all this

happened here I am 7 years later living the dream ... The sword is still with me though . The people in my house think it adds to the glory of the house so I have kept it . And we lived happily ever after .....

HOME SWEET HOME

END OF BOOK 1

9 798889 861102

Printed by Libri Plureos GmbH in Hamburg, Germany